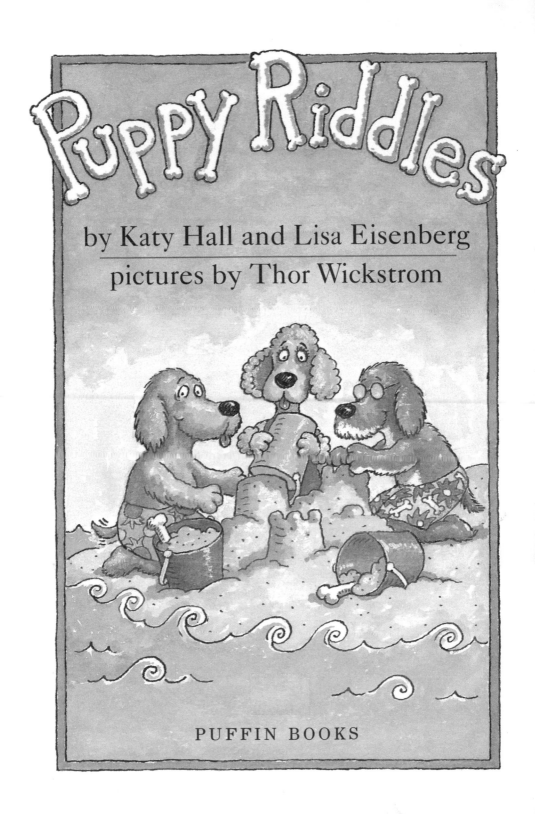

Puppy Riddles

by Katy Hall and Lisa Eisenberg

pictures by Thor Wickstrom

PUFFIN BOOKS

PUFFIN BOOKS
Published by the Penguin Group
Penguin Putnam Books for Young Readers, 345 Hudson Street, New York, New York 10014, U.S.A.
Penguin Books Ltd, 27 Wrights Lane, London W8 5TZ, England
Penguin Books Australia Ltd, Ringwood, Victoria, Australia
Penguin Books Canada Ltd, 10 Alcorn Avenue, Toronto, Ontario, Canada M4V 3B2
Penguin Books (N.Z.) Ltd, 182-190 Wairau Road, Auckland 10, New Zealand

Penguin Books Ltd, Registered Offices: Harmondsworth, Middlesex, England

First published in the United States of America by Dial Books for Young Readers,
a division of Penguin Books USA Inc., 1998
Published by Puffin Books, a member of Penguin Putnam Books for Young Readers, 2000

3 5 7 9 10 8 6 4 2

THE LIBRARY OF CONGRESS HAS CATALOGED THE DIAL EDITION AS FOLLOWS:
Hall, Katy.
Puppy riddles/by Katy Hall and Lisa Eisenberg; pictures by Thor Wickstrom.
p. cm.
Summary: A collection of forty-two riddles about puppies.
ISBN 0-8037-2126-9 (trade).—ISBN 0-8037-2129-3 (lib.)
1. Riddles, Juvenile. 2. Puppies—Juvenile humor.
[1. Riddles. 2. Jokes. 3. Dogs—Wit and humor.]
I. Eisenberg, Lisa. II. Wickstrom, Thor, ill. III. Title.
PN6371.5.H34865 1998 818'.5402—dc21 97-6375 CIP AC

Puffin Easy-to-Read ISBN 0-14-130575-4
Puffin® and Easy-to-Read® are registered trademarks of Penguin Putnam Inc.

Printed in the United States of America

The full-color artwork was prepared using pen and ink, colored pencils, watercolor, and gouache.

Reading Level 2.6

For Susie, Otto, Pixie, and Lucy
K.H.

For Tommy
L.E.

For Gertrude, Poochie, and Shark—
pups I have loved
T.W.

Aw, shucks!

How do we know that puppies love their dads?

They always lick their paws!

Where do little dogs
sleep on camp-outs?

In pup tents.

LASSIE COME HOME

ZZZZZZ...

8

Cannonball!

No kidding!

Why did the puppy jump into the river?

He wanted to chase the catfish!

9

What did the puppy do
when she won first prize
at the dog show?

She took a bow-wow.

Encore!

Bravo!

Hello. Care to buy some Flea biscuits?

What did the puppy
say to the flea?

"Don't bug me!"

11

What would you get
if you crossed a mutt
and a poodle?

A muddle.

What happened to the puppy who ate an onion?

His bark was *much* worse than his bite.

Why, Grandma, you've fainted!

Woof!

100 NASTY TRICKS TO PLAY ON YOUR FAMILY!

FiFi

Where do you take a sick puppy?

To the *dog*tor.

EYE EXAM CHART
H
OWMUCHI
STHATDOGGYIN
THEWINDOWTHEONE
WAGGLYTAIL? BO
NESWEETBONEB
EETBONE THATSMYFAV
ORITESONG BONESWEETBO

Now, say a-a-a-arf!

60 Paws

50 Paws

14

Where do puppies like
to go river rafting?

Collie-rado.

What song do little dogs like to sing?

"Pup Goes the Weasel."

...All around the cobbler's bench, the puppies chased...

Oh no, not again!

16

What do you call
a sunbathing puppy?

A hot dog!

What kind of soap should you use on your puppy's fur?

Sham-poodle.

18

What would you get
if you crossed a hunting dog
and a telephone?

A golden receiver.

Gotta get back to work, spot. I'll call you later.

19

What would you get
if you crossed an angry puppy
and a camera?

A snapshot.

Why did the puppy feel so frisky?

She had a new *leash* on life!

Durned frisky pup!

21

What would you say
if your puppy ran away?

Doggone!

Alas, farewell!

22

What do you call tough
little city pups?

New Yorkies!

23

Which puppy won the prize fight?

The boxer.

What kind of pups
did Count Dracula get?

Bloodhounds!

PETS

Pups

Bats

I vant to buy a dog!

Irish Setter

Wolfhound

Bloodhound

Pit Bull

Mastiff

25

What is it when a puppy
dreams he's fighting
another puppy?

A bitemare!

INTERNATIONAL PUPPY CONVENTION

Das ist Wunderbar!

I say! Smashing outfit, old boy.

German Shepherd

?

English Sheepdog

Which puppies come
from Spain?

Cocker Spaniards!

27

Which baseball team
do puppies play for?

The New York Pets!

What's the main ingredient in puppy biscuits?

Collie flour.

Lassie's Famous Biscuits
1. Fetch egg. Whippet.
2. Mix in arf a pound of Collie flour.
3. Add Pinscher of salt.
4. Bake until Golden.
5. Retriev'er. (use oven mutt)
6. Let setter. Chow down!

Old Bone SALT

Which vegetables
do little dogs like best?

Pup-peas.

Care for another helping, Fido sweetheart?

What kind of tree
do puppies like best?

Dogwood. They like its bark.

31

Let's have a _flea_ party!

Hey, pup! Come to our party!

It'll be fun, pup!

C'mon, pooch. There's plenty to _eat_!

Ha ha ha ha ha!

What's the difference between a puppy and a flea?

A puppy can have fleas, but a flea can't have puppies.

What would you get
if you crossed a puppy
and a kitten?

An animal that chased itself.

Yikes!

MEOWF! MEOWF!

33

What do you call a fancy
American puppy?

Yankee Poodle Dandy.

Why did the little dogs
hold paws?

They were in puppy love.

THE TUNNEL OF
PUPPY LOVE

35

What did the little dog
get for his birthday?

A new *collar*ing book.

What did the puppy say
when she stepped on
the sandpaper?

"Rough! Rough!"

What kind of stories
do puppies like best?

Furry tales.

Then the Furry Dogmother wagged her magic bone, and "woof!" Pupparella had a new gown!

PUPPARELLA

RAPUPZEL

The Dog Prince

The Princess and the Flea

38

...4, 5, 6, 9, 11, 14, 17, 19, 20...

Why are dalmatian puppies so bad at playing hide-and-seek?

Because they're always spotted!

How did pioneer puppies head west?

In waggin' trains.

West 957 Miles.

Welcome to
Puppy Track
Rules
1. No barking.
2. No drooling.
3. No running
around in squares.
Thank you.

Why do puppies run around
in circles?

It's too hard to run
around in squares!

41

What would you get
if you crossed a goldfish
and a puppy?

A guppy.

Why did the puppy go to jail?

He was caught barking in
a "No Barking" zone.

What does a mom dog say
when she wants her little ones
to quiet down?

"Hush, puppies!"

Fetch, Rufus, Fetch!

What did the puppy think
after he chased the stick a mile?

That it was far-fetched!

45

I can hear them, I just can't see them!

Baaah!

Baah!

Baah!

Which little sheepdog can't find her sheep?

Little Bo Pup!

Where do husky puppies like to sleep?

On a sheet of ice
under a blanket of snow.

...and through it all Buck staggered along at the head of the team...

THE CALL OF THE WILD

47

Oh, hello.

What should you do
if your puppy chews up
your riddle book?

Take the words
right out of his mouth!